THE CASE FILES OF HENRY CRANE
JACOB ALEXANDER

BOOK ONE
THE FALLEN AIRMAN

Chapter One
THE CALL

1942

There was a sense of displeasure in the way Henry Crane picked up the telephone; indeed, it was almost as if he didn't want to receive the call. Gingerly, he wrapped his thick fingers around the handset and lifted it to his ear. The weight of the thing laid uncomfortably in his hand. He still wasn't used to the home telephone he'd had put in. He had managed to have one installed before they stopped civilian production for the war effort. Crane knew so few people with a telephone, though, that he may as well not have bothered. He leaned back in the armchair and closed his eyes.

'Crane,' he said. The fingers of his free hand tapped a slow rhythm on the crest of the armrest. His voice was a rough, low growl. 'If this is a business call,' he continued, 'I might remind you that it's three in the morning.'

There was silence, on the other end of the line.

No, not quite... Crane could hear breathing, after a moment or two. A woman's, perhaps. Heavy, slow breathing, shuddering a little. He knew the sound all too well. It was a sound which usually meant one of two things; either the caller was at Hell's door and at the mercy of a particularly agonising death, or they were terrified out of their mind.

A business call, then.

'Hello?' he said softly. 'Who is this? Can I help you?'

'Hello,' came a timid voice from beyond the telephone. Hazy with the hiss of static, Crane could barely hear the woman, and he grimaced, pressed his ear right up against the receiver. Opening his eyes, he glanced toward the fireplace as he listened. Around him, shadows danced on the walls, flickering orange and grey in the light from the flames.

The room was far too large to be lived in, and so he had filled it with clutter; artefacts and paintings leant against every wall, propped up in every corner. Things that he had collected, things he had stolen. Things that had been given to him with trembling hands, hands that wanted nothing to do with those ancient objects and the terrible nightmares they contained.

Some, even Crane had been reluctant to take.

But the things were safest here, under his

protection. He had spent years of his life making sure this old house was the safest place in all of England; it was, in fact, the only reason he still lived here. Years of warding and protective symbols carved into the brickwork and the doors meant that, as long as he wished it, nothing could get in. And of course, the warding was strongest around this room, dug into every corner, every floorboard, every boarded window.

Nothing could get *out,* either.

Some of the artefacts and items bristled, as he sat there amongst them, with a kind of energy that he could only feel in those moments where the glow of the firelight played upon them. Some, however, emitted that same dark shiver constantly.

Some were, he felt, still *alive*.

A crackle of static from the other end of the telephone –

'It's my husband, Mr Crane,' said the woman, and Crane's attention was drawn back to the phone call. The woman's voice was barely a whisper, trembling with what he could only imagine must be fright,. Still, her words were fragmented by shivers, ragged breaths.

'Your husband?' Crane said. 'I don't know what you've heard, madam, but that's not the sort of work I tend to do.'

'He went off to fight, you see,' the woman continued, apparently choosing to ignore him. 'A couple of years ago. When the war started. And he...'

She broke off, then, into a fit of quiet, contained sobbing. Crane waited, eyes drawn to the knuckles of his free hand as they twisted to a rhythm he didn't care to recognise. The room was cold, suddenly, and he shivered. Turned his eyes to the flames in the hearth as they rose and fell. Something was waking up. 'Bollocks,' he whispered, standing up slowly. The telephone cord pulled at him and he scowled, scooping up the receiver and holding it against his waist. He tilted his head, nested the phone into his collarbone.

He was still dressed. He hadn't bothered to sleep. He couldn't, not while he was needed in this room. Not while *they* were restless.

After a moment, the woman on the phone continued.

'He came back to me, you see, Mr Crane,' she said, 'the other day. My husband came home.'

Crane shook his head, reaching for a poker by the fireplace, wrapping his fingers around the twisted iron handle. The flames crackled beside his face, throwing shadows over his jaw, over his bent, broken nose. A mess of sandy hair fell over his eyes as he turned.

'That's marvellous news,' he said into the phone. He glanced around the room, holding the poker aloft. Something had woken up. Something was watching him. If only he could *see* it... 'Truly great news, madam, but I'm not sure what this has to do with –'

'No, it isn't, Mr Crane, you don't *understand*,' the woman said. Louder now, indignant despite the timid edge to her voice. 'I received a telegram, a few months ago... it said... Mr Crane, it said... oh, God.'

'Yes?' Crane said impatiently. There, in the furthest corner of the room, he saw it. Movement, a flicker of shadow. And a sound, like the rustle of feathered wings –

'My husband is *dead,* Mr Crane.'

Crane froze. His grip on the phone tightened. In the corner of the room, the thing shuffled quietly, slipping between the shadows. Crane narrowed his eyes.

'I see,' he said.

'I have a friend...' said the woman. 'She told me that you helped her with... something. Something like this. She said you made it *go away.* Told me to ask for Mr Crane when I reached the operator. Please... can you help me?'

Suddenly the thing in the corner lurched forward, shrieking, raising curled, black claws and Crane swung the poker, propelled the tip forward with such force that the muscles at the back of his shoulder strained against the tendons holding them together, and the barrel of the poker smacked the shadowy thing in the belly and sent it flying –

Before Crane could move the thing had scrambled up and it reared up, screeching with a set of lungs too shrivelled and black to have contained that much air, and then it was lunging towards him, snapping its black-lipped jaws, pointed teeth clashing together and sinking into his leg, and he kicked upward, and the poker curled down towards the thing's face in a terrible, black arc –

Blood spurted as the thing's skull caved in, spattering Crane's trousers with thin, dribbling shreds of grey and pink. It stumbled for a moment on thin, spindly legs, toppled backward. Crane dropped the poker, panting.

The flames surged upward in the fireplace. The thing was dead.

Crane nodded after a second, wiping sweat from his brow with the back of his hand. 'Yes,' he said. 'Yeah, I can help you.'

Slowly, he looked towards an old grandfather clock in the corner of the room. The hands were twisted with age, the face scarred and scratched and bloody, flaking so badly that it was almost unreadable. Still, miraculously, it gave the right time. Three twenty-six. It was almost September, and the late summer nights were short. Soon, the sun would be up.

'Is he there now?' Crane said. 'Your husband. Is he there right now?'

'No,' the woman on the phone whispered. 'No, not now. It's just me and my children. George only... he only comes once a day. In the evening.'

'Interesting,' Crane said quietly. His eyes dropped to the dead thing on the floor, and he leant down to pick it up. Bloody flesh felt cold and leathery in his hand, and he winced, tossing the limp carcass onto the fire. 'What sort of time does he normally come?'

'It's... it's the same time every day, Mr Crane. Five forty-six. *Always* five forty-six. He comes to the front door, and he... he asks me to let him in. He gets... *angry*, when I don't.'

'Has he ever come inside?'

'No,' said the woman. 'I can't... I can't bear to open the door.'

'Good,' Crane said. 'It really would be a terrible idea to let him in.'

There was a pause. The woman's breathing had slowed a little, but still he could hear a tremble in the air; there was very little he could say that might calm her.

'I'll come by tomorrow afternoon,' he said, wiping his hand on the seat of his trousers. 'I'll be there just before five, okay? That'll give me enough time to set everything up. You should be safe until then.'

'I should be?'

'Stay indoors, if you can. I'm assuming you're calling from a house telephone?'

'Yes,' the woman said.

'Good. If you need me, call again. And if your husband shows up out of time... don't let him in.'

'Okay. Thank you for this, Mr Crane. Thank you so much. I'm so... I'm so *scared*.'

'I know. It's going to be okay. Now, where can I find you?'

Quickly, the woman told Crane her address, and he took it down on an old, battered pad he kept by the armchair. His handwriting was a horrendous scrawl, but it would do.

In the fireplace, flames crackled and whispered. Leathery skin bubbled.

'One more thing,' Crane said, stuffing the woman's address into his pocket, 'what's your name?'

'Helena,' she said. 'Helena Davies.'

'I'll see you soon, Helena Davies.'

Crane laid the handset back on its receiver and moved back to the armchair, settled in it comfortably. He reached for a crystal glass beside the phone and took a long drink. It burned the back of his throat, slipped down into his gut.

Crane looked one more time towards the grandfather clock. Three thirty-four.

There was no point trying to sleep now.

Instead, Henry Crane turned his eyes to the fireplace and watched as the flames danced wildly within, orange and white and gold, throwing twisted shadows on the faces of the things in the corners of the room.

He sat like that for a few hours, keeping a tired

watch of those things. Making sure they stayed where they had been placed, where they had been locked.

If anything else decided to wake up tonight, he would be ready.

Chapter Two
THE EVACUEE

It was almost noon by the time Crane pulled up to the station.

The car was a beauty - a brand-new, American model, the Mercury had been in his possession for barely a month, and already he had fallen in love with the thing. There was very little Henry Crane had found to love, over the years, but that car certainly made the list.

The paintwork was a deep, dark crimson that shone and glittered in the faded sunlight, gleamed so bright that it was a perfect, blood-red beneath the shade of the station wall. The tyres were slim and the hubcaps a shining silver. It seemed out of place, here, by the drab husk of the railway station. This far out into the countryside, there was no reason to keep up appearances. Especially not now that... well, there were other things to worry about, the last three years.

The engine cut out abruptly and Crane stepped out of the car, boots crunching over gravel thick with frost and scattered with the first fallen leaves of autumn. The seasons had been all wrong lately, he had noticed; now, barely on the eve of September, summer seemed to have finished and was making way for the death of the trees. Crane pushed the thought aside, pulled a grey overcoat tighter around him. He had changed out of yesterday's suit and dressed in a pale shirt and waistcoat and a narrow, grey tie. He rarely made quite such an effort, but he had to make an impression.

Henry Crane had been doing this job for a long time. Christ, he was the only one willing to do it. He had performed more illegal exorcisms than he could count - he had spent hours planning what he might do if the Church ever found out, but fortunately that was a bridge he hadn't yet had to cross - banishing rituals, healing spells... he had faced demons, spirits, witches, and yet...

Crane hardly felt fear, not anymore. He had grown so used to the paranormal, the otherworldly, that they barely affected him.

He was afraid now, though. This wasn't a ghoul, or a goblin, or some other unholy damned thing. This was *different.*

The railway station was a low, grey structure risen up out of concrete and corrugated metal, held together with rusted, iron rivets and thick, square bars. Once, it had been a fairly proud thing, a doorway between Crane's hometown in the country and the wider world, a tunnel connecting the vilage of Crowley to everywhere else. In the half-century it had stood there, though, nature had taken a good hold of the place;

thick, dark vines crept up the walls, sprouting poisoned brown leaves and thick thorns. Narrow trees hung over the shelter and sprayed their clawed, curled branches about it all. They were dying, slowly - soon, the curse of the season would strip them all of leaves and leave them curled, grey claws.

For now, however, the wild things had dominion over the station. Already the white-painted pillars were straining under the weight of the foliage that crawled around them.

Glancing up toward the trees, Crane walked towards the station entrance, hands shoved deep into the pockets of his overcoat. It was an old, tattered thing that his father had passed down to him, thick and grey and long enough that it swept the back of his knees with every step. It covered the blue tie and trousers that he'd worn for two days straight, as well as the bloodstain on the back of his white shirt. His black shoes were unpolished and the leather strained against tired, ragged laces; his sand-brown hair was a mess and the thin midday breeze threatened to push it into his eyes. He had forgotten, again, to shave, and the stubble coating his jaw was beginning to spread around his throat and itch beneath his collar. He reached up as he neared the platform, unfastened his top button. The tie fell loose around his neck.

Quickly, Crane moved up a set of wide, iron-grid steps and stepped up onto the concrete.

A quick look toward the end of the platform, to a flat, black clock mounted on the wall, told him that he was early. He had a few minutes before the train rolled in. Slowly, he walked along the platform, stood in the middle of it all. It smelled terrible, here, like bad eggs.

Sulphur.

The brickwork wall was lined with a set of white-rail benches, laid apart at equal intervals. Each one was empty - Crane was the only one here. Yet, there was movement...

Splashes of colour erupted from flower baskets hanging from the ceiling. Slowly, they swung in the breeze. Below the platform, the tracks were still beneath a fluttering of twisted, dead leaves. Crane shivered as a sudden chill passed over him. His breath appeared as mist before his face.

He sighed.

'Don't worry,' he said loudly. 'I'm not here for you.'

For a moment, silence.

He waited. A second wave of cold passed over him. He shuddered again.

'Honestly, mate,' he said, 'I'm just picking someone up. You can come out.'

Movement beside him. The shadows flickered, twisted in the air as it throbbed with cold and the bitter smell of sulphur grew worse, rose up from the tracks, mixed with something else, something that made him want to gag, something like rotten, dead meat.

'Who?' came a haughty voice from behind his shoulder.

Crane turned to face the newcomer, smiled weakly. 'You're looking well,' he said, nodding his approval.

The spirit scoffed at him. 'Sod off, Henry.'

The dead conductor spoke with surprising ease, considering he only had half of his upper jaw left and a mess of bloody teeth, bent outwards and torn apart. The rest of his jaw had been blown off with the shotgun round that he'd sprayed into his throat - most of the back of his skull was gone too, and if he stood at the right angle Crane could see right past him, view obscured only by dangling trails of pink and red that drizzled blood like running, fleshy taps. The leftovers of the spirit's head wer misshapen and bloody, twisted and sloppy at the base where his brains, grey and pink as the day he had killed himself, spilled down into his jacket. His throat was shredded, peppered with crimson holes. Blood oozed from some of them and pooled around his shirt collar. His eyes pointed in slightly different directions, black hair matted with red and stuck to his forehead. His conductor's uniform was stained and spattered with crimson.

He still had the shotgun in his hand.

The conductor held it steady, hugging it to his waist like a precious heirloom. All the times Crane had seen the spirit, he had never once let go of that gun. Crane had asked him, once, why he insisted on holding onto the thing that killed him. The ghost had raised an eyebrow - with great difficulty, in a manoeuvre that threatened to tear the rest of his face in two - and told Crane that if he could let go of the damn thing, he *pissing well would*, thank you. Apparently, whatever malevolent force was keeping him this side of the wall wanted the conductor to remember why he was dead.

'So who are you picking up?' said the conductor. Blood dripped from the back of his skull as if it were water dripping from a rusted old tap, and where it hit the floor in thick, red beads, it sizzled for a moment and faded into nothing. 'Not like you to bring *friends* home.'

Crane turned to the tracks, slid his hands back into his pockets. He was doing his best not to screw his face up in disgust; the appearance of the spirit was bade nough, but the *smell*...

'Don't push it,' he told the spirit. 'You're damn lucky I don't send you back to Hell, with all the *lip* you give me.'

The conductor shrugged. A chunk of flesh from the back of his mutilated skull dropped to the floor. For a moment it laid there, on the concrete, then it started to bubble and steam rose from it, and in seconds it had burnt to nothing at all. 'I ain't hurting anyone,' the spirit said. 'If you wanted to send me back, you'd have done it already.'

'It's nice to have connections,' said Crane. 'Speaking of... listen, what do you know about George Davies?'

'Who, now?'

'A soldier,' Crane said. 'He died a few months back. Well, that's when the wife received a telegram. You know what it's like, he could have been gone for a while before. Point is, he's back. You haven't heard anything, have you?'

The conductor grunted. 'Buggered if I know anything about that.'

'Christ, why do I keep you around?'

'Goodness of your heart?'

Crane glared at him.

'Oh, I forgot,' the spirit said. 'You don't have one, do you, Henry? You just -'

'Keep your mouth shut,' Crane said. 'That's enough.'

The conductor sighed. 'Look, Henry, the thing is... this war's a terrible thing. Worse than the last one, a lot of people are saying. No end in sight.'

'What's your point?'

'My point is, Henry, a *lot* of soldiers have died. Some of them are bound to come back. And I might know a little more than you about the way things work... here, on the other side... but I can't keep track of that many souls. Nobody could.'

'Fair enough,' Crane said quietly.

For a long time, there was silence. The two men stood side by side, eyes on the rail tracks; Crane pulled the grey coat around him, shifting his weight from one foot to the other as the cold ran through him. The spirit didn't seem to notice.

'I will tell you something, though,' said the conductor. Crane turned. He could see the spirit's windpipe through the holes in his throat - it trembled with every syllable. Crane grimaced as the conductor continued. 'More than usual, coming back through.'

Cane frowned. 'What do you mean?'

'The wall's getting weaker, Henry. Don't ask me how or why, but something's breaking it down. Piece by piece. You think you've seen a lot of us? There's a lot more coming, trust me.'

'Tell me everything you know,' Crane said.

'I don't know much. But I do know this,' the conductor said. 'There's a name, here, on the other side. A name nothing dead has any business saying.'

'What's the name?'

'It's -'

Crane leapt out of his skin as a whistle screamed behind him, long and low and loud, and then a rumbling, a shudder that echoed over the length of the railway track. The train was coming.

The conductor's crooked eyes widened. 'Bollocks,' he said. 'Must be off.'

Crane shook his head. 'No, tell me the...'

With a last, twisted smile, the conductor was gone, faded into the air, into nothing. The cold lingered.

Crane swore and turned his attention to the tracks. The train drew closer and began to slow, billowing great clouds of black steam from its pipes. It was a monster, still roaring even as it pulled to a stop, rattling a little. Smoke rose up around it in thick, black clouds. Crane stood back, sputtering in the fumes, waited for the thing to stop.

A door slid open, halfway down the second car.

Crane watched, face set, as the passenger stepped down onto the platform, carrying nothing but a small, brown package tied with string.

The train started to move away with a whistle and a blast of steam, a thunderous rumble echoing around the stationa as it pulled off. Eventually, the fog cleared.

Slowly, the girl looked up at him.

She must have been twelve or thirteen, dark hair pulled back from her face and pinned to one side, eyes equally as dark. She was wrapped tight in a thick, green coat, faded felt buttoned across her chest. She clutched the brown parcel tightly, as if she were afraid that if she dropped it she would never see it again.

'Hi,' Crane said awkwardly. He raised a hand, gave her a small wave. 'You're...'

He trailed off. His eyes flickered to the tracks, then back to her. He shrugged. Swallowed. There it was again - the fear. For a moment, he wished the dead train conductor were still standing beside him. Then, at least, the little girl would have something else to stare at.

'I'm sorry,' Crane said. 'I've never done this before.'

'It's okay,' the girl replied, smiling weakly. 'Me neither. I'm Claire.'

'Henry Crane. I guess you'll be staying with me for a while, yeah?'

The girl nodded. 'I hope that's okay.'

Crane smiled down at her. He paused. 'Two things you need to understand, before we go any further,' he said. 'First, of *course* it's okay. Whatever you need, I'll do my best. Alright?'

She nodded. 'Thank you.'

'Second,' he said. This one would be complicated. 'My work... actually, I'll explain that later. Let's get home, I'll show you round. Sound good?'

Claire smiled. 'Okay.'

She shivered as they walked towards the car. 'Why is it so cold here?' she said.

Crane swallowed.

Some things would take more explaining than others.

'Just the way it's built, I guess,' he lied, glancing

back towards the platform. 'Think the wind just sort of hangs about under the roof.'

As Crane walked away, the conductor waved him a slow goodbye, blood drizzling from his mangled face. At his side, the shotgun hung like a third arm.

Chapter Three
SPIDER

The evacuee barely spoke on the long drive from the station.

Henry Crane lived a fair way from the Crowley, and indeed the train station that connected the little settlement to London. For a while, they followed the main road, rolling smoothly over dark, flat tarmac. After a while, though, Crane turned the Mercury off the road and the tarmac turned to crumbling stone and then to rough, brown earth. Before long trees had risen up around them and they drove on through the thick of a stretch of dark, unhindered forest. The car bumped wildly over a winding dirt track through the middle of the woods, small shards of stone and dirt flying out from beneath the tyres.

'How come you're not fighting?' said the girl suddenly, as they reached the furthest depths of the forest. All around them, sunlight flickered and broke through the trees and canopies in fragmented shafts of white and gold, casting long, wild shadows over their faces. Crane squinted through the windscreen, tracing a slow path over the narrow track, guiding the Mercury with careful hands.

He paused for a minute, unable to reply. He could tell her the truth, of course, and in a small way he wanted to. He would have to, sometime. He could tell her *exactly* why he wasn't fighting, exactly what had happened...

But these things could wait. Besides, he thought, she wouldn't believe him. Not yet.

'I was too scared,' he lied, shaking his head. 'When they came for me, I hid. I ran away.'

'Okay,' Claire said.

Crane frowned. 'Okay? You don't think that's... weak?'

The girl shrugged, eyes on the road in front of them. It was coated in a layer of dark shadow and barely touched by the light from above the treetops. Still, she could just about make out the twisting shape of the path, the edges corroded and melting away into the dark undergrowth of the forest.

'No,' she said, 'who wouldn't be scared?'

'Cowardly, then, perhaps,' Crane said. 'You don't think I'm a coward?'

Claire shook her head. 'I think it's okay to be scared, sometimes. And I think everyone should be allowed to choose what they want to do.'

Crane was silent. Perhaps it was for the best that he had lied. She would discover the real reason in time, he was sure, but for now...

'So, is your dad fighting?' he asked.

Claire was silent. Crane glanced across at her as they curved around a tight bend, slowed the car a little. 'I'm sorry,' he said. 'I didn't mean to...'

'I never met my dad,' the girl said. 'He left, before I was born. He left me and my mum behind.'

'Oh, I'm sorry,' Crane said quietly. 'That's awful.'

Something moved in the backseat.

Claire cried out and turned, eyes wide. Crane slammed his foot down on the brake and the tyres squealed to a shaky stop on the dirt. He turned his head towards the thing -

'Oh, for Christ's sake, Spider,' he said.

Reared up from the shadows in the back of the car, the cat glared at him. Spider's black fur was soft and sleek and melted into the darkness, tail coiled high above his rump. His eyes glittered a fierce yellow. Softly, the animal purred.

'Christ, I'm so sorry,' Crane said, 'I didn't realise he'd come with me. He can be such a *little*...'

Claire was smiling.

It was the smile of a child, innocent and filled with pure joy, and Crane felt a pang of guilt at the sight of it. The things this girl would see...

'He won't bite,' Crane said slowly. He watched Claire with an ache in his chest. 'If you want to pet him. He might look like a vicious bastard, but he's all heart.'

'He's *beautiful,*' said Claire, reaching with a timid hand into the backseat. Spider backed away from the hand, glanced toward the driver's seat.

Crane nodded. 'She's good, Spider. She's a friend.'

The cat moved turned his gaze to the little girl. Slowly, gingerly, the animal moved forward, bowing his black head.

'Trust issues,' Crane explained. 'Once he gets used to you, he'll be okay.'

Claire grinned. 'I've never had a cat before. He's *lovely.*'

'Spider, come say hi properly,' Crane said. He turned, started the car again. Slowly he began to drive, ascending the winding track, and the cat slunk over the back of Claire's seat into the front of the car and sat on her lap, looking up into the girl's face as she stroked his head.

'Why is he called Spider?' Claire asked as they broke free of the forest and the track turned to a thin, flat gravel path. Light spread over the fields and the tall, swaying grass that surrounded them and the house rose up before them, beyond tall, grey walls and iron bars, and she didn't seem to hear his answer. Spider purred on her lap, already settled so that he was curled against her torso.

'Wow...' Claire breathed, staring up towards the house. Her hand had stopped moving and rested on the cat's soft shoulders, and he nestled into the crook of her arm, turned his yellow eyes to follow her gaze.

'It's really not as grand as it looks,' Crane said.

'You live here?'

'So do you, for a little while.'

'*Wow*,' she said again.

The house was tall and seemed a vain attempt to gain footing amongst the clouds; the east and west wings were matched with a perfect symmetry, proud with wide, glass windows and turretted, slanted rooves, separated only by a central mass of flint and stone, a great block of rough, patched-together grey that seemed to stand as the main portion of the house. All around the building were areas of uneven gravel and overgrown grass, contained within the tall, square walls around them, and beyond the house Claire saw more forest - tall, dying trees climbing toward the sky.

The house was, in many senses of the word, magnificent.

Crane pulled the car up as close to the front door as he could and stopped the engine. For a moment they paused, and Claire stared up at the building.

'How about a tour?' Crane said.

She turned to him and grinned. He gestured towards the house and the girl opened the car door hurriedly. Spider leapt off of her lap and hopped down to the gravel, looked up, waiting for the girl to follow. She stepped out of the car, clutching her brown parcel tightly. The cat followed eagerly as she walked towards the house, wrapping his slender frame around her ankles as she moved.

Crane hesitated.

After a moment, he stepped out of the car. Looked up, towards the sun. It couldn't have been much past noon.

Plenty of time, then, before he had to go and fix Helena's ghost problem.

'Welcome to Crowley's End,' he said quietly, and he followed Claire towards the house.

Helena Davies sat in the kitchen of a little terraced house, staring blankly into the depths of the room. With a trembling hand – it seemed to shudder almost constantly now – she stirred a mug of thin, watery coffee. Coffee had been a luxury, lately, that she had only been able to afford every couple of weeks. Coupons only got her so far, especially with two kids. Not that Elizabeth was eating much lately.

And Elijah...

The coffee had been cold for fifteen minutes or so, but of course Helena barely noticed. Last night had been terrible. One of the worst ever since George had come home. The smell of old meat hung around the house every time he visited, even though she never let him in, and it *lingered* through the night, so bad sometimes that she couldn't sleep at all. Last night, she had managed to scrape perhaps an hour and a half of unconsciousness from the dark. She hadn't expected Crane to answer the telephone at three in the morning, but she had simply needed to call him.

Something had to be done. It wasn't just her that couldn't sleep. Elizabeth would tell her mother that she was fine, despite everything, but Helena knew the girl was lying. Some night, she heard Lizzie crying.

And if she walked past Elijah's room she might hear him whispering to himself. Most nights now, up into the early hours. She would lean close to the door, put her ear up to the wood in an effort to hear him better...

The whispering would stop, then, and she would move quickly on to her bedroom. *Their* bedroom. To the bed where she and her husband had slept, where they had held each other on those long nights before he had gone to war. Before she had lost him.

The return of George Davies had been a pleasant surprise, the first time he had come to the door. She had seen his silhouette through the frosted glass and known, even before she opened the door, *known* that it was him. The telegram had been wrong, it must have been. After all, how could it have been right if he was right here? George was still alive. He had survived, somehow, and he was back. Helena could remember running to the door, twisting the knob with a trembling hand, ready to throw her arms around the man and tell him how badly she had missed him all this time, tell him how *afraid* she'd been -

Helena opened the door, grinning like a child.

Her smile disappeared. She *screamed.*

The man at the door was definitely her husband, there was no doubting that. But George Davies was quite clearly dead.

The first time, Helena hadn't known what to do. She had panicked. She stumbled back, and the dead man reached forward. Blood dripped onto the doorstep. She screamed again, shrieking louder than she ever knew she could, until her throat was hoarse, and then George was taking a step forwards, towards her, and she scrambled for the door handle and slammed it in his face. He might have been her husband, but she would not let him in. The way he had looked at her...

The first time, George had simply turned and left. Helena watched, through the frosted glass, through streams of hot, burning tears, clamping her hand over her mouth as the shadowy figure moved away from the door and disappeared, sucked into the air by some unknown force. He stumbled into the street, arms raised a little, and turned to take one last look... and then he disappeared. Crumbled into dust, into nothing.

As though he had never been there.

The next day, he came back. Five forty-six again. Helena came to the door, as she had the first time, but she didn't open it. She couldn't. George had stood there, on the step, and for a time he was silent. Then he stepped forward, and he pressed his palm on the glass, distorted and greasy and red with blood, and his head lolled forward so that his forehead rested on the wood. Helena could hear him, through the door, calling her name softly. And she turned, and she slid down the door and sat with her back to it, head buried in her hands, sobbing wildly as her dead husband whispered to her from beyond the wooden barrier.

The same thing happened for six days more. She came to the door every time, and she kept it closed. The bloody handprint faded, as soon as he took away his palm, but she couldn't pass through the hallway without imagining it there, on the glass. After a week of this, of being shut out of his own house, George began to grow angry when she wouldn't let him inside.

'*Helena...*' he would whisper.

'*Don't you love me?*'

Ten days, and George started hammering on the door. Pounding on the wood with both his fists, screaming and howling, shouting her name. She wondered if anybody on the street could hear her, but Crowley was a small town, and she was certain that if they could, they would talk to her. Nobody said a thing to her, and they smiled as if everything was normal, and she never thought to ask. Even if she could bring up the thing, what would she tell them? They'd think she was crazy.

'Helena... let me in, Helena. Helena. Helena!'

George only ever stayed a few minutes. Usually, it was all over in five or ten. An hour was the longest the barrage of screaming and thundering attacks on the door had lasted.

It had been the longest hour of Helena's life.

After a week more, George seemed to give up calling for his wife. The hammering grew louder, as did the old meat smell and the stench of rotten eggs that had joined it, and the house grew cold and damp with every passing day. Now, he called for his son.

'Elijah! Elijah! ELIJAH!'

George lost control, then, if he had been holding onto it to begin with, and his anger threatened to break the door. Helena barely left the house, and when she did she kept her head down, eyes on the floor. She was terrified that she might look up and he'd be there, watching, waiting...

Then she bumped into Claudia Harding, from across the street, and she broke down. Claudia invited her in, asked the woman to tell her what was going on. So they sat, in Claudia's kitchen, and Helena told her friend everything that had happened, and she prepared herself for the inevitable. Claudia would tell her she was insane, that she needed help.

No words came, and Helena looked up.

Claudia's face was stern, but sympathetic. She was

writing something in pencil, on an old scrap of paper. Helena frowned. 'What's that?'

'This is a name,' Claudia said. 'Someone who can help you.'

Helena shook her head. 'No, I don't want to see a doctor. I promise, Claudia, I'm not...'

Claudia slid the paper across to her. 'He isn't a doctor. Trust me.'

Helena read the name aloud. 'Henry Crane? I don't... who is he?'

'He helped me, Helena, when I had a problem like yours. He's helped a few people around here. Give him a call.'

Give him a call.

Helena looked up from her cold coffee and glanced towards a clock on the kitchen wall. It was getting on towards half twelve. A few hours, and Crane would be here. He would help her. Finally, it would all be over.

'Please...' she whispered.

Slowly, a tear rolled out from the corner of her eye and dripped into the coffee. Ripples spread across the top of the mug. The smell had long since faded. She wrapped her palms around the cup, but it was freezing.

'Mummy?' came a voice from the kitchen door.

Helena blinked, turned her face towards the voice. Elizabeth stood there, in the doorway, still dressed in her pyjamas. Helena hadn't let the little girl leave the house, these last few days. What if George never really went away? What if he was waiting, somewhere down the street, to take their child unawares?

What if he wanted Elizabeth to join him, down there in the underworld?

'Are you okay, Lizzie?' Helena smiled.

The girl shook her head. 'I want to go to school, mummy.'

'Tomorrow,' Helena said. 'I promise, sweetie. Tomorrow, everything's going to be okay.'

She looked back towards the clock, and she watched the seconds tick by.

Upstairs, in the room that had once been George's study, Elijah Davies was whispering to himself.

Chapter Four
CROWLEY'S END

'There's one thing I need you to understand,' Crane said, fumbling with the lock. The mechanism was stiff and rusted, and he ground the key forcefully into the door. A turn, and a push, and the lock clicked. 'One thing about this house you need to know.'

The old, oak-stained door opened with a long, drawn squeal and Crane grimaced. He stood straight as he turned to Claire and smiled thinly. The girl looked up at him with wide-eyed innocence and he hesitated, wishing he didn't have to warn her. Wishing, in fact, that she had been lucky enough to be signed an entirely different guardian.

'I'm sorry,' he said, shaking his head. 'One rule, and it's going to seem strict, but it's for your own safety. If I tell you not to touch something... Claire, don't touch it. Do you understand?'

She nodded meekly. 'Of course.'

Crane sighed. Closed his eyes for a moment. Around them, the breeze had picked up a little and the grey overcoat fluttered at his knees.

'Listen, Claire, there aren't going to be a lot of

rules. Not here. You're not my daughter, and as long as you're safe, and happy, you can do what you want. But there are things in this house that I need you to avoid.'

'Okay, Mr Crane.'

'Don't... don't call me Mr Crane. Henry, yeah?'

Claire smiled. 'Henry.'

'Alright,' Crane said, and he found that he was smiling too. 'Now, if you'd like to step inside...'

'Why do you have dangerous things in your house?'

Crane swallowed. 'Because the only person they can hurt in there is me. Well, usually. Now... now they can hurt you too, obviously. If you *touch* them. But don't blame me for that, blame the Nazis for bombing us all.'

'Am I safe here?'

Crane swallowed. 'Of course you are. As long as you follow my one rule, you will be safer than you've ever been. This place can be scary, and the things in here... they can be scary too. But I promise you, Claire, on my life and the lives of everyone I have ever loved, you are going to be safe here. And when the war's over, I'll send you home in one piece. I promise you, you are *protected*.'

Somehow, Claire was still smiling. 'I believe you.'

Crane nodded.

'Let's go. I'll show you where the kitchen is,' he said, leaning back against the door to hold it open. He gestured the girl inside and bowed his head. 'And keep your shoes on, the floor's filthy.'

Claire stepped through the door and Crane closed it behind them. It was almost as cold in the front hall as it had been outside, and the lights were off. Something brushed against his ankles as he reached for a switch beside the door. He hoped it was the cat.

Crane flicked the switch and a dim, orange glow flickered from the bulbs hung around the room. Long, dark shadows retreated into the corners of the hall and Claire stepped forward, the black cat at her heels.

'Main hall,' Crane said quickly. He gestured wildly toward the centre of the room, swept his arm across it all. He forced a smile. Largely, it was empty. The cracked, concrete slabs that made up the floor were covered, in places, with thin rugs, but there was no furniture, save for a row of hooks by the door. Cobwebs swung lazily from the corners and the lights, twisting about their brass fittings, thick with dust. Crane frowned at the dust. Perhaps he should've cleaned up a little before he headed for the station.

'How big is this place?' Claire marvelled. She didn't seem to have noticed the cobwebs.

Crane shook his head. 'No idea. Too big for me. But it's safe,' he said. 'That's all that matters.'

Claire walked slowly through the hall, shoes clipping quietly on the concrete. Her eyes flew from one wall to another, from the half-open doors to the peeled paintwork.

'I'm sorry,' Crane said. 'You should've been placed with someone better -'

'I love it,' Claire breathed.

Crane frowned. 'It's a *dump*.'

The girl looked over her shoulder, one eyebrow raised. She grinned. 'You're funny.'

Crane bowed his head a little, gesturing towards the first door on the girl's left. 'Kitchen?' he suggested, but she shook her head. A smile flashed across her face.

'Show me the dangerous things.'

Crane's eyes flickered to another door, one the other side of the hall. It was open, just a little. Firelight flickered beyond, dampened by shadows.

He hesitated. 'Are you sure? You never have to go into that room, Claire. You never have to see them.'

She followed his gaze, looked toward the door. 'Is it safe, to go in there?'

'Well, not at nighttime.'

'Why not?'

'Because that's where I sleep.'

Claire's eyes moved to the back of the hall, where a great, twisting staircase writhed and swirled upwards to the second floor, all thick banisters and wide, marbled platforms. 'You don't sleep upstairs?' she asked.

Crane didn't answer.

'Show me,' Claire said, turning back to face him.
'Please?'

Crane nodded. 'Your room, first. Let's get you settled in.'

He slung his coat onto a hook by the door and moved across the hall, walking quickly, eyes forward. Avoiding the lure of that door, that room. It could wait. It *had* to wait. Right now, Claire was just a child. Innocent, naive, separated from her mother by a war she had no part in. Stuck in a stranger's house until it was all over. But *right now*, that was the worst of her problems.

As soon as he opened that door, that would all change.

The two of them climbed the stairs quickly and Crane led the girl across a narrow walkway that jutted from the wall, supported by narrow, curved pillars. A wooden rail was the only thing stopping them falling to the concrete floor of the main hall, and Claire looked over the rail as they walked, taking in everything. As they reached the end of the walkway, Crane opened a door on his left and beckoned her through.

'Yours is just down the end,' he said. 'It's my old room, so you'll have to excuse any mess.'

'There's blood on your shirt,' Claire said, behind him.

Crane blinked.

'Just there,' she nodded towards his gut, 'are you okay?'

Crane looked down. 'Oh, that. That's... yeah, no, you're right. That is blood. Not mine, though, don't worry.'

Claire frowned. 'Are you a policeman?'

Crane opened his mouth to answer. He closed it again. After a moment, he shook his head, nodded towards the corridor beyond the open door. 'Go on,' he said. 'Go take a look.'

Claire moved forward and Crane frowned, looking at the brown package she was clutching, the tiny parcel containing everything she'd brought with her. 'Are you having clothes sent over?' he said.

The girl looked up at him. 'This is all I've got,' she said quietly.

'Ah. That's okay,' Crane smiled. 'We'll see what we can find, alright? Anyway, go on. See what you think.'

He watched, hands shoved deep into his trouser pockets, as Claire started walking down the corridor. Her steps were slow and cautious, echoing a little off the flat walls. She stopped at the last door on her left, turned her head towards him.

'Go on,' Crane said.

With her free hand, Claire opened the door and tepped inside. Crane waited a second then turned his attention to the bloody shirt, licking his fingers and rubbing the material furiously. Of course, it had soaked in. 'Bollocks,' he hissed. Footsteps. He looked up. Claire stood in the corridor, shadows over her face. She was no longer carrying the little brown package.

'What do you make of it, then?' he said.

Claire nodded quietly. She said nothing.

Crane shook his head. 'If it's no good, I can sort you something else. Sorry, I didn't know what to... is everything okay?'

She smiled weakly. 'The room is lovely,' she said. 'Thank you. It's really nice, Mr Crane. I just... I really miss my mum.'

Crane swallowed. 'I know.'

'I think she would like you,' Claire said, nodding a little. 'She would be happy I'm here.'

'Let's go into town tomorrow, yeah? Send your mum a letter or something, let her know you're okay. I mean, I've got a telephone downstairs, if you want to...'

He trailed off. Claire was crying.

'Come on,' he said, reaching out a hand. 'Let me show you the living room. We'll figure everything else out later.'

Claire moved towards him, floorboards creaking beneath her feet. She looked at his hand for a second, then she reached up and wiped away her tears.

The girl took Crane's hand, and he led her down the stairs.

'Remember, don't touch anything. Your life might

depend on that.'

The living room, like many of the rooms in Crowley's End, sparsely decorated. An armchair, the chair in which Crane would sit, most nights, and fade in and out of sleep, was all that burdened the carpet. The fireplace was decorated with an assortment of pokers and twisted, black shafts, but the hearth was empty of a coal scuttle or basket. There were no tables, save for the small affair beside the armchair, upon which Claire could see a new-looking telephone. The dial gleamed in the firelight. There was no wardrobe, no desk.

Instead, the room was filled with *things*.

There was no other word, she felt, as she stepped inside, that might describe the assortment of objects and items in here. There seemed to be no pattern to them, or to the way they were arranged; indeed, many of them were simply discarded on the floor or leant against the wall, which was painted a pale, fading blue. There must have been hundreds of things, big and small, all shapes and colours. Thousands maybe.

'What are they?'

'Relics,' Crane said slowly, watching her from the doorway. 'Artefacts, fossils, ornaments. Anything you can imagine.'

'Are they old?'

'Some of them. Some are thousands of years old.

Some are brand new.'

'Why are they here?'

Crane paused. This moment, right here, was when everything would change. What he told the girl next would ruin her life forever, he knew that. It was inevitable. He *had* to tell her. She had been sent here, by powers beyond him, by a government that seemed intent to sacrifice everything they could if it meant winning the war. She was unfortunate, that was all. Unlucky enough to end up with Henry Crane as her guardian and protector. This wasn't his fault.

That was what he would tell himself.

If he didn't tell her the truth about this room - about *him* - Claire would be in danger as long as she was here.

'My work,' Crane began, moving into the room, 'it's complicated. Christ, it's *very* complicated. My job... I don't know how to explain this to you.'

Claire looked up at him. The firelight played over her face. She needed to know.

'I'm an investigator,' he said. 'That's the easiest way of putting it.'

'A detective?'

'Kind of. But the things I investigate... well, does the word "paranormal" mean anything to you?'

The girl shook her head.

'Alright. See, I'm a paranormal investigator. And that means I investigate things which aren't supposed to be here.' He paused. 'Claire, do you believe in ghosts?'

She shook her head again. 'Ghosts aren't real.'

'Oh, this is going to be hard,' Crane said to himself. 'What about demons? Goblins? Tricksters, maybe. Anything.'

'Demons are real,' Claire nodded. 'Demons live in Hell, with the Devil.'

'Sometimes,' Crane said. 'Sometimes, though, they get *out*. And if that happens, Claire, I'm the person who has to send them back. Same with the dead, the damned. Anything that comes through from the other side. I'm the one who finds them and puts them where they belong. Well, I'm sure there's others like me. There must be. But I look after Crowley, and this part of the country. It's my job to protect you from the things that go bump in the night.'

'I don't understand,' Claire said.

She turned her eyes back to the room, to the assortment of things in there. In one corner, illuminated by the firelight, was a tall lamp on a shining steel pole. The shade was crudely stitched together with crimson thread, a patchwork of thin, veined leather. The bulb inside flickered a deep blue, so dark that it was almost black, and the light seeped out from beneath the leathery shade like mist.

The lamp wasn't plugged into the wall, didn't flicker like flame. Still, it glowed. At the base of the lamp, a child's toy was coiled around the pole, a stuffed, ragged snake with green felt for skin.

The snake's eyes had been torn out.

The lamp was surrounded by things Claire couldn't begin to explain, things she didn't *want* to be able to explain. A wooden cross was laid against the wall, tilted so that it was almost upside-down, stained dark and rotted away.

A porcelain doll was stuffed inside a cardboard box, taped over so that only her black, glass eyes were visible. Another box, hidden behind what could only be the lid of an old coffin, had something scrawled on its side:

Another box, the other side of the room, was open and overflowing with a collection of weapons; Claire saw a knife with a black, wide blade, encrusted with something like salt; a long, coiled rope, frayed at one end, tarred and stiff and wound around itself like the stuffed snake; a thin, curved sword with a handle inlaid with shining jewels.

On the wall above the fireplace, a mask hung by a crooked nail. It was the face of a jackal, perfectly carved out of black-stained, thick wood. Its eyes were perfectly hollowed out, and its sharpened, black teeth were set into bright red, wooden gums.

Its pointed ears jutted from a crown of thorns.

'Everything in this room,' Crane said, his voice drawing Claire's attention from the mask's empty eyes, 'is haunted, or possessed, or cursed. Or *alive*. Some of the curses are dormant. Some are practically harmless.'

'What about the others? The ones that aren't harmless?'

'The house keeps them... *quiet*,' Crane said. 'It's a special place. It's protected. But still, you can never touch anything in here, okay? Promise me that. That's my one rule, and I need you to keep to it.'

Claire nodded.

She wanted to tell him that he must be lying, that ghosts didn't exist. She had never believed, and why should she now, just because of some old, creepy things? Why should she believe?

But her eyes kept falling upon that lamp, in the corner, the blue flame concealed by leathery skin, a flame so dark it could only have been stripped from the night itself.

And all the while she was looking at the lamp, the jackal's head above the fireplace stared down at her...

'How can you sleep in here?' she said quietly. She felt something, deep within her gut, that she hadn't expected to feel. It wasn't fear, although she felt that too. It was *excitement*. There was something special about Crowley's End. The house, and this room...

'I have to,' Crane said. 'I have to keep an eye on eveything. If anything ever got out...'

Claire nodded. She paused, as if she was thinking about something. Crane supposed she must have a lot of questions. He certainly would.

'What do you want to know?' he said.

Claire looked up at him. 'What do I tell my mum?'

Crane hesitated. 'Whatever you want. If you tell her about this, she'll have you sent home again. I wouldn't blame her. And you'd never have to think about these things again, or about ghosts, or demons... or about me. But understand this, Claire. You are safer in this house, right now, safer with me, than you will be back in London. What's going on, now, with the Germans... this house is *protected*. We won't ever get bombed here. I don't know if I can explain why, or if I should, but this is the safest place on earth. And everything in this room... well, you never have to go in here. I keep it locked, when I'm not around. Stay away from this room, and you couldn't be safer.'

Claire turned to him. 'Mr Crane, I'm scared,' she said.

All the bravado had gone, all the curiosity and courage that had spurred her on towards this room, and for a moment Crane was reminded that she was just a child. Just a little girl.

'I'm sorry,' Crane said, 'but right now, scared is the best thing you can be.'

Chapter Five
THE GHOST TRAP

It was almost five o'clock, when Henry Crane pulled up on the side of the road.

Helena lived in a little terraced house, halfway along what could only, in a town as small as Crowley, be called the high street. All this term meant, of course, was that it was the largest street in town, but it was home to no more than two dozen houses and a post office. There was a corner shop, a little way down the road, but it was open so rarely now that it was hardly worth taking note of. It was far safer here, though, than it would be in the city; in the whole of Crowley, there had only been one bombing since the beginning of the war, and just a single fatality.

In a town as small as this, you were more likely to die from suffocation than anything else.

Crane stopped the car and cut out the engine. It juddered to silence and he sat for a moment, taking in the street. Above him, the sky was empty, a haze of grey muddled with thin, pale clouds. The road wide enough, just about, for two cars to pass by each other, but along the whole street Crane only saw one other, parked outside a house a little way along from Helena's. Other than that, three or four bicycles. Probably some kids'. Most people seemed to prefer the train. Well, Crane supposed, there wasn't a whole lot of sense going anywhere far these days.

Still, it felt to him as though Crowley was slowly dying, and there was nothing he could do to stop that.

Crane stepped out of the car. Spider had stayed behind to keep Claire company. He seemed to like the girl, and Crane was glad. He didn't want her alone in that house, not yet. But he couldn't have brought her here.

Out here, unprotected by the foundations of the house, by the warding that he'd spent so many years painting beneath the wallpaper, carving into the very framework of the building, a spirit was one of the most dangerous things in the known world.

And he had promised to keep her safe.

Crane crossed to the back of the car, reached inside to gather his things. He swung a faded leather satchel over his shoulders, slipped an iron blade into his belt. A slim, wooden crucifix had fallen into the footwell and he reached down to grab it, stuffed the thing into his coat. Finally, he wrapped his arms around a tall, wireless radio that he'd leant down in the backseat and hefted it up to his chest. Gripping the thing tight, he carried it awkwardly out of the car, kicking the door closed.

Helena was already standing outside her front door when he turned around.

'Ready?' he asked her quietly. She nodded, opened the door with a faltering smile.

'Come in.'

Crane crossed the front garden, treading quickly over a narrow, dirt path that led through the clipped grass. Three flat, concrete steps led up to the door, painted a pale, pastel green. Helena stepped inside and he followed her in.

Immediately he noticed the cold inside the house, shivered as he set the wireless down by the door.

'Do you want me to take your coat?' said Helena, nodding toward the tattered old thing around his shoulders. She was pretty, he realised, prettier than he'd imagined when he'd first spoken to her. Her black hair fell in thick tangles around a pale face and she had dressed smartly; grey skirt to her knees, dark blouse. He smiled, shaking his head a little.

'I'll leave it on for now. Thank you,' he said. 'Has it been this cold since George came back?'

'The cold?' Helena said. 'Oh, this house has been cold for months, but it started getting worse when he came back. Why do you ask? Is it him?'

'It could be. But usually, any atmospheric changes disappear when the spirit leaves. This cold seems to be hanging around.'

Maybe George had a little more presence than

Helena realised.

Crane shook his head, smiled. 'Just you in the house today?' he asked.

Footsteps, then, behind the woman. He glanced down as she stepped aside and his eyes met those of a little girl with blonde, straight hair. She was dressed all in pink, with white socks that came halfway up to her knees.

'I guess not,' Crane said.

'This is my daughter, Elizabeth. Say hi to the gentleman, Lizzie.'

'I'm seven,' said the girl innocently, smiling up at him. 'Are you here to send my daddy back to Hell?'

Crane blinked.

Helena turned, bent down so that she was on the girl's level. 'Lizzie, that's enough. Why don't you go fetch Elijah, ask him to come downstairs?'

Elizabeth nodded, turned excitedly and ran up the narrow stairs in the hall. The house was small, compressed into a few tightly-packed rooms, and from the hallway Crane could see into the kitchen, into a tiny pantry beneath the stairs, and across the other side of the hall, a square living room. Shoes lined the wall one side of the door, coats hung above them; one each. Pink, green, grey.

'Nice place,' Crane said, smiling at the woman.

'Can you do it?' Helena said abruptly. 'Can you make him go away?'

'Yes.'

'So tell me about yourselves,' said Crane, fiddling with the wireless. He had set it up on the kitchen table, right in the middle of the wooden surface, and Helena's family had gathered around the thing with some kind of distracted fascination, waiting to see what it would do. Elizabeth had sat at the head of the table, leaning upward so that she could see over the lip. Helena sat at the other end, and Crane between them, with his back to a cracked, ceramic basin.

Across the table from him, view largely obscured by the bulk of the radio, was Elijah Davies. He had inherited his mother's black hair, evidently, and it fell over one side of his face in a half-combed mess. He was dressed in a smart shirt and a buttoned cardigan, all shades of grey.

He was all too skinny, for a boy his height.

'Let's start with you, Lizzie,' Crane said, turning to the little girl as he pushed his hand into the depths of the wireless, twisting wires about themselves with steady, absent-minded fingers. He had done this so many times now that they almost worked on their own, moving with little conscious instruction.

The girl grinned, teeth flashing beyond her round cheeks. 'Okay. What do you want to know?'

He smiled. 'What do I *need* to know?'

The girl shrugged. 'I like ponies, I guess. And

school.'

'You like school? I *hated* school.'

Helena shifted uncomfortably in her seat. Crane clocked the movement and turned back to the wireless. A little more wiggling, and the wires were in place. They hummed, just a little. Crane finished inside the wireless and replaced the back panel, muttering something under his breath, almost chanting the words. The humming grew a little louder. Static brushed over his fingertips. He stopped, turned to the little girl one more time. 'So how come you're not at school today, Lizzie?'

'Mummy won't let me go,' Elizabeth said. 'She says I have to stay inside until daddy's gone home.'

Crane glanced towards the woman and they shared a silent look that said everything. There was fear, in her eyes, an intense kind of terror that he had seen all too many times. 'Very sensible,' he said quietly. 'Your mummy seems like a very clever lady.'

'What's the wireless for?' Elizabeth said.

'Oh, you'll see,' he smiled. 'So Elijah, how come you're still about? Boy your age - what are you, sixteen? - I'm surprised you haven't run off to go fight some Nazis.'

Helena raised her eyebrows, answered before the boy could open his mouth. 'Don't put stupid ideas in his head, Mr Crane,' she snapped. 'I'm not losing my boy again.' She reached across the table, laid a hand on

Elijah's shoulder.

Crane paused. 'Again?'

'Elijah ran away,' Lizzie said.

'I didn't *run*,' Elijah protested. 'I...'

Crane nodded. 'It's okay,' he said slowly. 'Where did you go, Elijah?'

'I... I just...'

'It doesn't matter,' Helena said quickly. 'You came back, Eli, and that's all that matters. You came back to us.' She smiled at him and looked up, towards a clock on the wall, hung above the doorway. 'It's nearly quarter to six, Mr Crane. What do we do?'

Crane paused a while before answering. His eyes never left the boy's face. There was something strange about Elijah, something he couldn't quite put his finger on. And his mother didn't want to talk about it, which made it all the more important.

'We wait, for now,' Crane said after a moment. 'There's very little we can do before it... before your husband shows up. Until then, there's just a couple of questions I need to ask. Is that okay?'

Helena nodded, tension spreading across her shoulders. 'Yeah, that's okay.'

'Alright. Good. Firstly, do you ever notice any strange smells in the house?'

Helena nodded slowly.

'What kind of smells?' Crane asked.

'I don't know, maybe... eggs? Like really bad, *bad*

eggs.'

'It smells like meat, sometimes,' said Elizabeth. Crane nodded.

'Okay, that's good. That's usual. Means this is definitely a spirit we're dealing with.' Crane turned the wireless around so that the speaker was facing him, looked into the meshwork grille. Shadows shifted beyond, inside the thing. They were all set. 'How long do these smells linger, after he's gone?'

Elijah shook his head. 'It always smells like that.'

Crane looked up. 'I'm sorry?'

'Not always,' the boy said. 'But it comes and goes. Nighttime, it's usually pretty bad. But morning, afternoon... it doesn't get worse when he comes to the door. It's *always* there.'

'Okay, that's interesting. And Helena, you said it had been cold for a few months now.'

'Just a problem with the heating,' she nodded. 'We've had people come look at it, but... no, it's always cold here. Not just when he comes to the door.'

Crane nodded. 'Usually, the presence of a spirit comes with signs. Omens. Clues, I guess, is one way of thinking about them. Cold spots in the house, certain smells. Rotten meat is a common one. Burning oak, sulphur, sometimes.'

'Bad eggs?' Elizabeth said.

Crane nodded. 'Something like that. But if the smells are lingering, if it never gets warmer... well, that could mean that George is sticking around longer than you realise. Last question, Helena. Do things ever *move*? Maybe when you're not looking. Certain objects, do they move around? Maybe you leave your keys somewhere and they turn up later in a different room.'

For a moment, the room was filled with an uneasy silence. Crane raised an eyebrow.

Elizabeth raised a timid hand.

'Go on.'

'Sometimes,' she said slowly, 'my wardrobe... the doors open by themselves, sometime, and they close again. Like something's in there.'

'Anything else?'

Another pause. Tension had gathered in the room, and it hung like the cold in the air.

'Mum,' said Elijah quietly. 'You should tell him.'

Crane turned to Helena and saw that she had started crying. He reached across, laid a hand on top of hers. 'It's okay,' he said, 'you can tell me. You *need* to tell me.'

She shook her head.

'Elijah?' Crane said. 'Will you tell me what happened?'

Elijah hesitated, looking towards his mother. Her hand went to her mouth, but she wouldn't look up from the floor. A tear rolled down her cheek.

Elijah nodded. 'Yeah, it... a couple of days ago.

Me and mum were inside. Lizzie was out in the back garden. Mum told me to go check that she was okay. I went to the garden and... I came back, and the telephone wire was wrapped around mum's neck. She was screaming and... she was trying to get it off, but it kept *squeezing,* and tightening, like it was trying to... like it was trying to kill her.'

Suddenly, the wireless began to hiss. Helena yelped, crying out as the noise grew in intensity, grew louder. A whisper of static, nothing more, but then something beyond the static, a voice...

'*Elijah...*'

Crane smiled. 'Nearly time,' he said softly. 'He'll be here soon.'

'Oh, God,' Helena said, face raw with tears. 'What do we do?'

'We get ready,' said Crane. 'I'm going to need some salt and a knife, Helena.'

'What for?'

The smile grew wider.

'We're going to set a ghost trap.'

Chapter Six
THE DOOR

The cat joined Claire in her room, after a little while. They curled up together on her bed, and after half an hour or so Claire began to talk to the animal, stroking his back softly with the palm of her hand.

'I like him,' Claire said. 'You must like him too, if you stay here. You don't look like a house cat. You're a stray, aren't you? Maybe he found you somewhere. He likes collecting things. Maybe you're another thing.'

Spider didn't seem particularly offended by this, so the girl continued.

'Maybe we should go exploring. Would you like that? After all, I've only seen a few rooms. If we don't touch anything, we'll be okay. Mr Crane didnt say we couldn't do that, did he?'

Spider sat up, tail curling slowly from side to side.

Claire stood from the bed and the cat leapt down to join her as she crossed the room to the hallway. 'Where do we go?' she said. 'Maybe we could go outside, see what the garden's like. Or...'

Her gaze moved from one end of the corridor to the other. At the near end, the landing led to the stairway and back downstairs.

At the furthest end, a big, grey-painted door stood closed and silent. The door was cloaked in shadows, almost as though they were making a conscious effort to conceal it. It was a heavy-looking door, with a big, brass knob, set into a dark frame. The floor around it was coated in dust. Cobwebs hung across each corner.

'Let's see where this goes,' Claire said quietly, and they turned and headed for the grey door. Her footsteps echoed on the floorboards as they creaked beneath her. The sound bounced off the walls, the soft patter of Spider's own movements far quieter than the clip of her shoes.

Claire stopped, when she reached the door. It was warm, here. Hot, even. As if there was something burning, the other side of the door. Slowly, she raised a trembling arm.

She gripped the doorknob tight and twisted it, pushed.

Nothing.

The door was locked.

Claire frowned. Shrugged. 'I guess we can't go in there,' she said. 'There must be a...'

She trailed off, eyes falling to the floor.

The boards were littered with shallow, rough scratch marks, as if something had been trying to get in. Curls of sawdust loitered in the gouges, left over from whatever tool had been used to carve the wood.

The scratches were set in threes. Like sets of fingernails, or...

'Don't be silly,' she said to herself. She spoke quietly, almost afraid something might be listening. Some*one*. 'What has three fingers, anyway?'

But she couldn't help herself. It didn't look like any tool had made these marks. Some of the rivets were coated with a thin red dust. Dried, but still recognisable as blood.

Behind her, the cat seemed hesitant to come any closer.

'Someone really wanted to get in here,' Claire said quietly. She looked closer - the marks didn't end at the door, but continued beneath it, through it to the other side. 'Or... maybe someone really wanted to get *out*.'

She shivered and stepped back. Behind her, Spider had turned around and was padding towards the landing. After a moment, she whirled round to follow the cat downstairs.

She would save exploring the house for another day. For now, the garden was calling.

The garden at Crowley's End was bigger than Claire could have imagined, and she spent a full hour wandering every lawn, every cracked pathway, circling every patch of overgrown grass and thicket. Most of it lay behind the house, separated into squares of thick, green grass and dark foliage, bordered by narrow walkways and cement patios.

At the furthest end of the garden, a dark forest rose up from the ground, autumn trees reaching for the clouds in some mad display of hopeless projection, all curled, dead branches and grey bark.

Claire found herself heading for the trees, after a little while, crossing a mess of thorns and weeds that met her waist, swept about her thighs. The cat walked with her, but often disappeared into the wild flora. At times, the only sign that he was still there was a flicker in the dry, brown grass or a rustle in the scrawnier bushes.

The girl found a thin, winding gravel path and followed it to an opening in the first layer of trees. She turned back, looked towards the house. It looked smaller, from here, and she wondered just how big this place was, how far she'd walked just to get from one end of the garden to the other.

Her eyes travelled upwards, following trails of ivy up the brick and the sharp, grey flint that made up the back of the building. There, halfway up, a small window that she fancied must have been the window of her new bedroom. Yes, she recognised the colour of the walls. Caught a glimpse of the corner of the old, brown wardrobe.

And there, a little way to the left of her window, another. She saw nothing behind this one, just a thick, dark black. A fluttering shadow, like an old, ragged curtain.

This must have been the room beyond the grey door.

Claire swallowed nervously, turned back to the forest. She plunged into the dark, and Spider followed, and soon she was quite lost in the thick of the trees. It was just as overgrown and unkempt in here as it had been out on the lawn, and difficult to navigate, but she found that there was a clear path, leading somewhere; old, dead branches on the ground had been trampled and cracked underfoot; mud and filth was littered with bootprints; here, caught on the curved hook of an overhanging branch, was a fluttering strand of brown hair.

The girl followed the path a little way, and the forest grew darker, and she looked above her. Light filtered through the criss-cross of branches, pale, grey sunlight. It was fading fast.

Moving quicker, she kept her eyes down, looking for prints, for trails. Whoever had been down here hadn't bothered to clear up after himself. She could only assume it had been Crane.

He was a funny man, but she liked him.

Of course, she would have to tell him, at some point. About herself. About her mother. But that could wait. For now, she was learning about *him,* about who he was, what he did. He was a ghost-hunter, an exorcist. Or so he said.

Claire had very little reason to believe that ghosts existed, but he was so convinced. So *determined* in his passion for it. Perhaps there was something in it after all...

After all, Claire had never felt the way she did when she looked at that mask, in the man's living room. As if the wooden jackal with the bloody maw and the hollow eyes was looking right back at her...

Claire stopped. The path ended.

Here, buried in the depths of the forest, there was a glade. A small circle, about the size of her room, surrounded by silver trees with thick, crooked trunks. This was the only place she'd seen, so far, that wasn't untended. The grass was clipped and green. Beads of dew clung to the blades as they fluttered in a light wind.

In the middle of the glade was a grave.

A crude, wooden cross had been planted in the ground and stood at a funny angle, just slightly off straight. The two planks had been hammered together with a pair of rusted, iron nails. The wood was cracked and sore.

Claire stepped forward slowly, knelt by the grave. Spider stood beside her, tail drooping between his legs.

There was a plaque, on the ground. Carved out of thick, grey stone.

Claire's breath hitched in her throat as she read the

names etched into the plaque, and she laid a hand over her mouth. Suddenly, it seemed very cold indeed.

Claire stood up, looked down at the black cat. Spider returned her gaze, blinked a pair of softly-glowing yellow eyes.

'We should go,' Claire said quietly. With one last look at the grave, she turned back to the forest and ran.

Chapter Seven
17:46

Salt was in short supply, these days, but Helena seemed to have amassed a fair amount in the bowels of her kitchen cupboards, and Crane soon set to work spreading a thin line of the crystalline powder across the kitchen doorway.

'What's that for?' Elizbeth asked, standing behind him in the hall.

Helena was marking the front door with a stick of charcoal from Crane's satchel, copying from a design that he'd given her scrawled on a scrap of notepaper, while Elijah scratched the same symbols into the floorboards with the tip of a kitchen knife.

'Salt's pretty good for stopping spirits,' he said. 'They can't cross over it, see? So if we have a line here, across the door, he won't be able to get into the kitchen. You with me, Lizzie?'

The little girl nodded excitedly as he stood up and handed her the bag.

'Want to help us out?' he said, and Elizabeth nodded again, grinning.

Crane smiled back. 'Alright, you take this into the kitchen, yeah? Find every window, every opening. Every crack in the wall. And just put a little line of salt across it. Like I've done here, yeah?'

'Yeah,' Elizabeth said, running into the kitchen. Crane stepped back into the hallway.

'How are we doing out here?'

'Nearly done,' said Helena from the front door. Indeed, the charcoal symbols were starting to take shape; curves and elegant, twisted shapes spread over every panel of wood, coming together to form a series of sigils and symbols that looked amost like letters, the alphabet of some ancient, dying language that couldn't be understood.

'Good,' he said, 'Elijah?'

The boy nodded, crouching on the floor. He had lifted up a corner of the bare rug that was laid there and was carving intently, leaving shallow traces in the boards. He didn't say anything.

'Alright, nearly there. Elijah, I'm going to need the knife back when you're done, yeah?' He looked up into the kitchen, towards the clock on the wall.

'Nearly time,' he said quietly.

'Why is it always that time?' Helena said. 'Always five forty-six. Always. Why is that?'

'It's a good thing,' Crane said. He shoved his hands into the pockets of his overcoat, nodded towards the door. 'There's a wall, between the spirit world and ours. A barrier, if you like, separating the living and the dead. Stronger spirits can pass through at will, pretty much. Some can come and go, stay as long as they like. Stay forever, unless they're sent back through. Or *dragged* back through. Some, though - the weaker ones - can only pass through at certain points, certain times. When the wall is a little thinner, a little weaker. So it might be that a certain spirit can only pass through on a certain day of the year, maybe stick around till the next day. Then he's pulled back through. Make sense?'

'But why that time? Why five forty-six?'

Crane paused.

'Most often, the wall gets weaker at the moment of passing,' he said quietly. 'Your husband probably died at five forty-six, which means that's the only moment he can break through the wall.'

Helena nodded.

'But that's good news,' Crane said, a little more cheerfully. 'That means he's a weak spirit. Easier to send back.'

'He's still my husband,' Helena whispered.

'No,' Crane said. A darkness flashed across his face. 'No, he's not.'

He stepped closer to her, careful to avoid stepping on the patterns that Elijah had carved into the floorboards. 'I'm sorry, Helena,' he said, 'but George stopped being your husband the moment he died. It takes a lot to pass through that wall, even for a few minutes. A lot of strength, willpower. And the easiest way to gather that much willpower is to get angry. Really, *powerfully* angry. Mostly, the dead stay dead, and that's because it takes so, so much out of them to come back. Your husband is a vengeful spirit, Helena. He's not George Davies anymore. To become that angry, that *furious*... enough to break through the wall... it will have taken his soul. And I'm sorry. But we really need to send him back.'

He turned, moved to the kitchen doorway. Inside, he could hear the wireless hissing softly.

'Why can't you just bring him back to me?' Helena said. Crane stopped moving.

On the floor, Elijah looked up. The knife was frozen in his hand. Particles of sawdust floated from the tip to the ground, dancing in the air as they drifted downward.

'It's been done before,' Crane said. He looked across at her, right into her eyes. The darkness that had flickered across his face fell over it now, dull and calm in his eyes. 'When we send him back, it's permanent. Whatever gate he's passing through to cross the barrier, we close it behind him. And it is possible to close it while he's on this side.'

'So let's do that,' Helena said. 'Let's bring him back here.'

'Helena, he's not your husband. We can bring back

most of him, but not his soul. Not his character. He'll just be everything that he is now. Angry. Violent enough to break through the wall. He'll be trapped, and that'll make him worse. He will *kill* you and your children, given time.'

Helena was silent. Her eyes fell to the floor.

'I just want my George back.'

'I know. But he's not your George anymore. I'm sorry.'

She nodded, hand moving to her mouth. Behind Crane, Elijah stood up. The boy handed Crane the knife and moved across to the doorway, held his mother tight.

'It's okay,' Elijah whispered.

Crane slipped the knife into his coat and watched as the two of them stood there, sobbing quietly. Behind him, the wireless hissed and hummed, bristling with static whispers. Elizabeth appeared in the kitchen doorway, smiling as she lifted the bag of salt up to his nose.

'I'm all done,' she said, and he smiled down at her.

'Good girl. Now, you go in there and stay safe for me, yeah?'

'I want to help, Mr Crane. What can I do?'

'Tell you what, Lizzie. You keep an ear on that wireless, alright? You *listen.* And I want you to write down everything you hear. Do you think you can do that for me?'

She nodded. 'What if I don't hear anything?'

Crane stood up straight, looked toward the door. 'I don't think you'll have to worry about that,' he said.

Elizbeth stepped through into the kitchen and Crane reached into the satchel at his waist, wrapped his fingers around something small and round, something that burned his hand a numb, intense cold. He pulled the pendant free of the bag and looped the iron chain over his head, tucked the thing into his shirt.

'Come on, then,' he whispered. 'Helena, Elijah, I need you to wait in the kitchen.'

Behind them, someone knocked on the door.

'*Elijah...*'

A shadowy figure appeared, beyond the frosted glass. Helena cried out, stepped away from the door. Elijah backed away slowly. The newcomer knocked again.

'Now, Helena. You don't want to be here for this.'

'What are you going to do?'

'I'm going to let him inside.'

'Are you insane?' Helena cried, staring wide-eyed at the man. 'You said that would be a bad idea, you told me not to -'

'Of course it's a bad idea,' Crane said. 'It's a *terrible* idea. Helena Davies, this is th most dangerous thing, right now, that we could *possibly* do.'

'Then why are we doing it?' Helena yelled. Behind her, George knocked again on the door. Hammered on it with the crest of his fist. The doorframe shuddered.

'*Elijah...*'

'Why is he asking for you, Elijah?' Crane said suddenly. 'Why *your* name?'

Helena shook her head. 'He started with mine,' she said, speaking loudly over the pounding of fists on the wood of the door. 'It was all he would say. Then he started... screaming it. I still didn't answer. I guess he thought Elijah might listen to him.'

'Elijah, what do *you* think?' Crane said.

Elijah said nothing, eyes on the door.

'*Let me in...*' came the voice from beyond the door, a low, rasping whisper.

The hallway was suddenly very cold.

'*Elijah...*'

'You can't let him in,' Helena said. 'Please, Mr Crane. You don't have to let him in. You *can't*. You can't let him take my boy away, not again.'

'Get in the kitchen,' Crane said, moving towards the door. 'Both of you.'

'Mr Crane -'

'*Kitchen*, now!'

Helena backed away. She watched the man for a moment, as he moved his hand to the doorknob, then she turned, headed for the kitchen table. Elizabeth was furiously scribbling onto a piece of paper, words she might not even have understood. The wireless was hissing loudly, a stream of static barely concealing strings of voices, fragments of conversations -

'Elijah, I'm going to need you to go too,' Crane said.

The boy didn't move.

'Elijah!'

George was still knocking, relentless in his passion, it seemed, to break down the door. '*Elijah...*' he said from the other side, banging on the wood with a ghostly fist. The shocks of every impact echoed around the hallway.

'Elijah, get out of here,' Crane said, as calmly as he could, eyes on the boy. 'He wants you. Only you. If you stay where he can get to you, he *will*. You need to *go*.'

Slowly, Elijah moved away, never taking his eyes from the door.

Crane hesitated, hand resting on the doorknob.

'Let's see what's got you so angry, shall we?' he whispered.

He opened the door.

George Davies stood on the doorstep, hands raised to break the door down.

For a moment he was still, apparently stunned that, for once, the door had opened.

George was still dressed in his uniform - buttoned fabric the colour of old, dead moss, fabric so thick and stiff it looked as if it were holding him up. His form flickered and faded in and out as he stood there, crumbling at the edges, reforming and shifting and changing. Twisting violently as though something were trying to pull him away, to suck him right back into thin air.

He was quite clearly dead.

Blonde hair, slicked back with wax, was matted with grease and filth, the same dirt that coated his face and his clothes. A dusting of soot laid over the moss-green pads of his shoulders and his jaws. He looked like he'd crawled straight up from the trenches to get here. A pale beard coated the lower half of his face and thin trails of blood drizzled down from the corners of his mouth, where it bubbled between his lips, frothing, rising up from his broken lungs. Slowly, he smiled.

A fat, dark bullet hole stared out at Crane like a round, black eye in the dead man's chest. The uniform around the wound was frayed and bloody, and beneath it Crane saw a soaked, white vest turned bright red. Through the hole, beyond strings of gristle and sinew, he could see the other side of the street. There was another hole at the man's shoulder, a deep trail where a bullet had grazed him, left him raw.

A third had taken his left eye, left it a black, hollow pit. Grey-pink oozed from the edges of the socket, beads of liquified brain trickling down his cheek.

'*Elijah...*' George whispered, stepping forwards.

Crane stumbled back a step, hand moving to the pendant at his neck.

It hummed softly as he whispered, chanting quietly, matching the passage written on the door and carved into the floor, repeating word for word, again and again...

'*Come to me,*' the spirit said. It was looking past Crane, now, at something behind him in the hallway. But Crane had told Elijah to go into the kitchen. The boy had left. Hadn't he?

George took another step, moving slower as the chant continued. He flickered and faded, weakening every second. The ritual was working.

'*Elijah...*'

'You can't have him,' Crane said, shaking his head. The pendant burned cold at his chest. The chant was over. The spirit was weak. All it would take was one final push...

George looked right at him. The spirit's eyes were cold and dead, whites pale and milky and melting into irises that had been stripped of their colour, fading into tiny, black pupils.

'Elijah's protected,' Crane said confidently. 'You can't reach anybody in that kitchen, George.'

The spirit smiled. Its eyes flickered to that same spot in the hallway, just beyond Crane's field of view. Crane turned, looked -

Elijah was frozen there, just feet from the kitchen,

eyes on the dead man.

'Elijah, *move!*' Crane yelled. 'Get into the kitchen!'

'I can't...' Elijah whispered. His face was crippled with an expression of fear, his legs trembling. 'I can't move. I... why can't I...'

'*Elijah...*'

Crane turned back to the spirit, hand moving once again to the pendant, but he was too slow. A ghostly hand rose to his face and curled, bloody fingers dug into his face, etherreal claws burning his cheeks, burying themselves in his eyes. Crane yelled in agony as a wave of pure cold washed over him, ice flowing through his veins -

He collapsed, crumbling to the floor, and the soldier's spirit passed by him, moving quickly, with purpose, reaching for Elijah -

'Elijah, get away from him!'

The boy glanced towards the kitchen, but something was stopping him. He turned on the spot, raced up the stairs, bounding up them two at a time, but he wasn't fast enough, and George was following him -

'Bollocks,' Crane said, staggering upwards. He grabbed the knife from his pocket, held it aloft as he crossed to the stairs.

'I thought the trap was meant to keep him here!' Helena yelled from the kitchen, her voice a shrill cry.

'Well, it's keeping him in the house!' Crane

replied, nearing the top of the stairs, his chest pounding. The pendant sang around his neck. 'Apparently it's not floor-specific...'

At the end of the landing, Elijah had his back to the wall and was sobbing wildly, hands pressed to the paintwork, eyes wide. A small painting hung on the wall above his head, a still life. Three oranges in a bowl. It was hideous.

George was bearing down on the boy, bloody fists raised, cursing the boy in some foreign language, but not an old language - French, perhaps, some strange dialect Crane hadn't heard before -

'*Leave the boy alone*,' Crane said, raising the knife. The pendant was *screaming* at him. *Do it,* it yelled, *send him back. Send him back!*

Slowly, the spirit turned. George's smile grew into a thin, red scar across his bloodied face. His form had stopped flickering altogether now. He was stronger. It would take a little more to send him back through. It could take a *lot*.

'*You can't hurt me,*' the dead man said.

'I know.'

Crane raised the blade of the knife to his free hand and cut a deep, red line across the palm. The spirit frowned, opened its mouth to question, to protest, but already Crane had tossed the knife to the ground and was grabbing at the pendant with his bloody palm -

'*No!*' the spirit screamed.

The pendant burned Crane's hand and he closed his eyes tight against the pain, grimaced as hot, white fire spread through him, passing into his blood and *out* again, and then there was a sound like death itself, a sound that echoed about the whole house, and his eyes snapped open.

'*Ad Infernum,* soldier!' he yelled, and the spirit shrieked, fading in and out, throbbing and pulsing in the air, hands glaring bright red with blood as its remaining, soulless eye started to burn white, and then the dead man was consumed, all at once, by a writhing mess of silver and blue and gold, traces of fire flickering amongst it all, and then he was gone.

Blood dripped to the floor. Crane fell to his knees. Behind him, footsteps, pounding up the stairs. Helena Davies was sobbing wildly, reaching for the son she had come so close to losing for a second time. But it was all over now.

George was gone.

Claire burst out of the trees and bent over, hands on her knees, catching her breath. Her shoes were clogged with filth and the thorns had scratched at her calves and she grimaced, looked up. The moon had risen a little further now, and it was almost fully dark.

Beside her, Spider emerged from the foliage, shook himself off. His black fur was slick with dew. His eyes glimmered, a damp firelight behind each one.

His ears were perked up.

Claire stood straight, nodded towards the house. 'We should go back inside...' she started, trailing off when she saw it.

The window.

The room behind the grey door.

Where before, the room had been in complete darkness, now it was lit, glowing with an intense, orange light that flickered and pulsated behind the glass. Shadows moved in the firelight, and Claire shook her head.

'That's not...' she started. 'That's not possible.'

She looked down at the cat. 'It's just us in the house, isn't it?'

Spider stared up at her, said nothing.

Claire looked up again.

The light had gone out.

'I must be going crazy,' she breathed, and the two of them headed back for the house.

Chapter Eight
LET ME IN

'Claire, everything okay?'

Crane pushed the front door closed, shrugging off his grey overcoat. The satchel fell to the floor.

There was no reply.

He turned, began crossing the hallway to the stairs.

'Claire? Sorry, the job took a little longer than I thought! You alright?'

Nothing. Silence reigned in the empty house. He moved to the living room, peered inside. Everything was still. The jackal mask hung silent above the fireplace. Watchful. The flames, ever lit, had not dulled.

Nothing had moved.

'Claire?' he called, a little louder, turning again. Maybe she was asleep.

Movement on the staircase. He glanced across to the stairs, smiled. 'Hey, boy.'

Spider was perched there, halfway up, tail wrapped around the banister. The cat's eyes glowed a faint yellow.

'Where's she gone?' Crane said quietly.

The cat stared at him for a moment, eyes blank and motionless. Then, as if in answer, it raised its head, nodding towards the top of the stairs. Crane smiled his thanks and began to climb. Spider followed him up.

Crane knocked on the girl's door before he entered her room. He heard a sniffle, followed by a faint cough. 'You can come in,' Claire said, and he opened the door.

The girl had been crying. She sat on her bed, hastily wiping her eyes on the back of her wrist. 'Sorry,' she said quietly, 'I didn't hear you come in.'

'Don't apologise,' Crane said, moving to the bed. He sat beside her, laid a hand on her shoulder. 'Are you missing home?'

She nodded. 'I'm sorry.'

'Hey, it's okay. It's okay to miss home. Your mum, I'm sure she misses you too. Do you want to call her?'

'Not today,' Claire said. 'I don't want her to know... I want to wait until tomorrow.'

'Okay,' he smiled. 'That's fine. But any time you like, you let me know and we'll give her a call. Does she have a phone?'

'Yeah.'

'Then we'll figure something out, don't worry. Have you eaten anything?'

Claire shook her head.

'Alright, well let's fix that problem first, yeah? I think I've got some bacon, there's a loaf of bread down there somewhere. The one thing they'll never ration. Then we'll go into town tomorrow and use up some coupons, get us something nice. That sound like a plan?'

Claire nodded, smiling. Eyes on the ground.

'Hey,' Crane said, 'it's going to be okay. I promise you. It'll all be over soon, and you can see your mum again. She can always come down here, if you want her to. Come and visit you?'

'That would be nice,' Claire said.

Crane stood, gestured toward the door. 'I'll go cook something up, alright? You stay here, if you like, I'll bring your food upstairs.'

She nodded, looking up at him as he turned to leave.

'Mr Crane?' she said.

He looked back. 'Henry,' he said, 'please.'

The girl hesitated.

'What's behind the grey door?'

Crane froze, just for a moment. Then he smiled. 'Oh, that's where Spider sleeps,' he said. 'He's got a whole wing to himself, the spoiled little sod.'

'The door was locked,' Claire said.

'He's a very clever cat,' Crane replied. 'He likes to find his own way in.'

Claire smiled.

Crane turned, closed the door behind him. He looked down and his eyes were met with a fierce, yellow glare. Spider's tail had coiled into a thin, black spiral.

'I know,' he said, as they walked toward the stairs. 'But at least it was a *white* lie.'

Darkness settled, and Spider joined him in the living room. Claire had gone to bed early, and after a little while Crane had checked up on her. Already, even before the moon had risen above the trees behind the house, she had fallen asleep. Well, it had been a hell of a day for her.

'You know, we should get her mum down here for a weekend or something,' Crane said as the cat curled up over his feet. He reached for the glass on the coffee table, took a long drink from it. 'Sometime soon, yeah?'

The cat was silent. Across the room, a blue flame glowed beneath an old lampshade. Above the fireplace, bathed in the flickering orange glow of the flames, the jackal's head stared at them.

Crane reached into his pocket, pulled out a sheet of crisp, yellow paper. He had almost forgotten about the wireless, about the ghost trap. 'Let's see what we've got here then, shall we?' he said.

Elizabeth's handwriting was difficult to read, but

still just about legible, and Crane's eyes darted across the paper. She had done exactly as he'd asked, taken down everything she had heard.

Most of it was just fragments, pieces of conversations from the other side of the wall. Some of it was George. The rest... well, Crane had found that even from this side of the barrier, if a radio was wired up exactly right, if it was charmed, then things could slip through. Voices.

He had always imagined that the audio transfer from the other side was one-way. Now, though, looking at the words Elizabeth had written, he swallowed.

Perhaps they could hear him, too.

He wondered who might've said that. George certainly hadn't. So someone, on the other side of the wall, had been watching. Listening. Perhaps it was a spirit he'd met before. Or one he might meet in the future.

The wall was a complicated thing.

Whoever – or whatever – had spoken, it was clear to him now that the conductor had been right. The wall was getting weaker.

Something terrible was coming.

He frowned. Something about the transcript didn't make sense. Or rather, it made too much sense, as if it were part of a conversation between two spirits - seldom had he encountered two souls in contact with each other, and he paused over the dialogue. It must have been a coincidence. Surely...

Something was wrong, here. Elijah had been standing behind him when the spirit had been knocking at the door, and Crane hadn't heard the boy say anything at all. Maybe it was just another spirit, another piece of some conversation from the other side of the wall. Maybe it was just bad timing.

Or...

'No,' Crane whispered. 'It can't be.'

Suddenly the phone was ringing beside him and the paper dropped from his hand, floated to the floor. At his feet, Spider sat bolt upright, and Crane reached for the handset. raised it to his ear.

'Helena,' he said, before she had even spoken. 'What's happened?'

'It's Lizzie,' Helena cried, voice breaking through streams of sobbing. The line crackled terribly. 'Please, Mr Crane, you have to come and help her. There's something here, something in the house. Please, it didn't work! He's still here, somehow, George is still here – oh, God, you have to help us! Mr Crane! Mr Crane?'

The telephone swung lazily from its wire.

Crane was already gathering his things.

Chapter Nine
AD INFERNUM

The door was open when Crane arrived. It was dark. He stepped out of the car and rushed up the garden path, stumbled inside. 'Helena!' Outside, the moon had risen and hung in the sky, a perfect circle of white.

'Upstairs!' she called, from somewhere in the house. Her voice was hoarse. 'Hurry!'

It was cold in the house, colder than before, and there was a smell in the air, a *stench* like old, dead meat stripped form the bones of rotten carcasses and burned with salt and sulphur, so bad that it *burned.*

Crane glanced about him – the hallway was a mess. The protective symbols in the floor had been torn up with the boards, and he leapt over them, lunged toward the stairs. He sputtered as he ran, covering his mouth with the palm of his hand. He reached the top of the stairs, turned, onto the landing - *there*, slumped on the floor.

Helena was breathing heavy, her back against the wall, head tilted back.

'Help her...' the woman whispered. With a limp

hand, she pointed towards a door off to the right. Her fingers were bloody. Her face was as pale as the moon. Her clothes were torn and spattered with red.

Crane burst through the door and into Elizabeth's room, reaching for the pendant at his neck. 'Elizabeth!' he yelled. 'Get away from the window!'

But something was holding her there, forcing the little girl's timid frame against the sill. Her hair fluttered in the wind as she screamed. She held on tight, gripping the windowframe with all her strength, but the window was open and something was pushing her towards it, pushing her head down -

Crane rushed forward and wrapped his arms around the girl's waist, pulled back.

'*Elijah!*' he yelled. 'You need to stop this!'

Behind him, Elijah appeared in the doorway. 'I don't understand,' he said. His voice was soft, slow. Dazed, almost.

The wind howled at Crane's face and he cried out, straining against the force pulling Elizabeth towards the window. 'Let her go!' he said. 'She's your sister! You don't want to do this!'

'Help me!' Elizabeth was screaming. 'Please, don't let me fall!'

'*Listen to her!*' Crane yelled. 'Elijah, *stop this!*'

Elijah moved forwards. The boy's face was blank. 'It's not... me,' he said. 'I'm not doing this. It's dad... he's come back. You didn't send him away...'

'Oh, I did,' Crane hissed. 'But now I know, Elijah! Now I know why it was your name he was calling, why he only wanted *you!*'

Suddenly the grip on Elizabeth loosened and they flew back from the window, crashing to the ground. Crane turned, crawled forward, reaching for the pendant -

'It's not me,' Elijah said. 'How can it be me? I'm...'

He stopped. Crane shook his head.

'I'm...'

'No,' Crane said. 'You're not. And I am so, so *sorry.*'

Behind him, Elizabeth had curled up into a ball and was covering her head, rocking from side to side. Helena appeared in the doorway, crawling on her hands and knees, hair a tangled mess. She fell. Crane moved to her, reached to pick her up, but Elijah was there first, laid a hand on his mother's back.

'It's okay,' the boy whispered.

'No,' Crane said. 'It's not. Don't listen to him. Helena, your son is *dead*.'

Helena looked up, her eyes wild. 'No,' she sobbed. 'No, he can't be. He's... he's right here.'

Crane began whispering, chanting the same ancient language he'd cited before. In his hand, the pendant seethed as though it were angry. The air grew colder still. Behind him, the window slammed shut with such force that the glass shattered into thousands of tiny pieces, spraying the room in a shower of clear shards.

'Your son ran away,' Crane yelled over the sound. 'When George went off to fight, when *Ellen* died -'

Helena shook her head, sobbing. All around them the air hummed, burning with all the ferocity of a thunderstorm. 'How did you know about Ellen?' she cried. 'I never -'

'All the clothes in here, they're all too big for Elizabeth,' Crane said, nodding to the open wardrobe. The doors flapped, open and shut, and dresses and dungarees and floating, knitted jumpers rippled. 'How old was Ellen when she died, Helena? Twelve, thirteen? And that was always going to hit Elijah hard, losing his little sister.'

'So I ran away,' Elijah yelled above the howling wind, standing up, swaying a little. 'So what?'

Crane paused. The wardrobe doors slammed shut, stopped. 'Tell them where you ran to, Elijah,' he said. 'At the age of *fifteen*, tell your mother where you ran.'

'I can't do that,' the boy said, shaking his head. The wind picked up and now glass dust was swirling around them, carried by the breeze, whistling and rising and falling with every breath of air.

'Elijah, tell me!' Helena said, looking desperately at the boy.

'They need to understand,' Crane said quietly.

Behind him Elizabeth was sobbing into her lap,

face buried there and wrapped in her arms. The wardrobe opened again and the doors crashed open, slammed shut. Open, shut, open, *shut, open...*

'*I went to war!*' Elijah cried. 'Okay? I did what dad did, and I signed up to *fight!*'

'Elijah...'

'You lied about your age,' said Crane. 'They taught you how to shoot, and how to fight... but it wasn't enough.'

'I don't understand,' Elijah sobbed. 'I fought so hard. But... it was too much. So I came home. I...'

'Oh God...' Helena whispered. Her hand went to her mouth.

'You *died*, Elijah,' Crane said. 'Earlier, when I told you to get into the kitchen, you couldn't. You told me you didn't know why. I'm sorry, son, but it wasn't because you were scared. You couldn't cross the *salt line*. I am so sorry...'

Elijah shook his head. 'I'm not... I didn't...'

'Maybe it was gas. Poison. That would explain why it's so hard to tell. But you came back home, what, a few months ago? Exactly when it started to get cold. And the smell, the smell that lingers even when your dad's ghost isn't here? Sometimes, the dead don't *remember*. But Elijah, you have to make it stop. *Look at her.*'

Elijah's eyes flickered to his sister, huddled in a corner of the room. The child was still screaming, even now.

'I didn't...'

'I'm sorry,' Crane said, 'I really am. But I have to do it.'

Helena stood on shaking legs, moved forward. 'No... I can't lose my boy again...'

'I'm so sorry, Helena. But he never really came back.'

'No,' she said again. 'No, no, no, please. Maybe we can just... please...'

'I'm sorry.'

Crane turned to Elijah and opened his mouth to begin the final line of the spell.

There was a hand at his arm. He looked down.

Elizabeth stared up at him, eyes full of tears.

'I can't let him stay,' Crane shook his head. 'I'm sorry. Maybe he won't even know he's doing it, but what happened tonight, it'll keep happening. He'll keep lashing out until you're both dead.'

'I know,' Elizabeth said. 'I want to say goodbye.'

Slowly, he nodded.

She ran to her brother and wrapped her arms around his waist. Silently, Elijah looked towards his mother. Helena looked to Crane, and then to her boy, and she crossed the room to join Elijah and Elizabeth's tight embrace. The three of them stood there for a long time, holding onto each other, eyes closed.

Weeping together.

Crane waited a while before he touched the pendant. When he spoke, it was not with the usual confidence. Perhaps they could work it out, if he let the boy stay. Perhaps, once they knew, it could be okay. For a little while, at least.

But he knew it couldn't be. Not for long.

'*Ad Infernum,* Elijah,' he whispered. Then, under his breath, choking up, he uttered the last line of the spell again. '*Ad Infernum. Back to Hell.*'

The boy gave Crane one last look, a look that said everything. Then he crumbled into dust and the particles in the air disappeared, and Helena and Elizabeth were left holding each other, an empty space between them.

'I'm sorry...' Crane said quietly. For a moment he stood there, deflated, defeated, and then he turned to leave, moving past them into the hallway. He descended the stairs without a word, wrapped the coat tight around him as he crossed to the front door. Outside, the wind had dropped.

It was warmer, now, inside the house.

Footsteps behind him. He turned.

Helena wiped tears from her eyes. 'Thank you,' she said.

'Please,' Crane shook his head, 'don't thank me. Not tonight. Not after...'

'You did what you had to do,' Helena said. 'And I *hate* you for it. But... I understand. George wasn't my husband anymore. I guess... I guess Elijah wasn't really my son, either.'

'Maybe not, in a way. But you will always have what they were before. *Remember* them.'

She nodded. Paused for a moment, as though she had something more to say. She shook her head.

'What is it?'

'It's just... you said something before, about needing... *strength* to cross the wall. Have *you* ever been through it? To *their* side?'

Crane smiled. 'Goodnight, Helena.'

She nodded. 'Fair enough. And can I ask... how did you know about Ellen?'

'The clothes, upstairs...'

'No, her *name*. How did you know her name?'

Crane smiled weakly. 'Lucky guess,' he said. 'I noticed a pattern.'

Helena nodded, smiling back at him. 'Thank you. Do I... do I pay you?'

Crane turned to the door, shaking his head. 'Not for this,' he said. 'Not for what I've done tonight.'

He crossed the hall to the front door, reached for the handle. His hand hovered over it for a moment. After a second, he turned back.

'I'm sorry, actually... maybe there *is* something. You've kept all of Ellen's clothes. Do you... do you have plans for them?'

Helena frowned. 'I guess I just never got round to

throwing them away. Sentiment, you know? But now that it's just... oh God, now that it's just me and Elizabeth...'

'I'm sorry,' Crane said. 'I shouldn't ask... but maybe you don't have to get rid of them,' Crane said. 'There's a girl, staying at mine... an evacuee. Claire, she's called. She's twelve years old. Maybe, if you don't want to throw them all away...'

Helena smiled weakly. 'Of course. Better than burning them.'

'Thank you.'

'But how did you know Ellen was... gone?' she asked. 'How did you know she hadn't just... *moved away?*'

Crane thought back to the transcript, to Elizabeth's scrawled handwriting.

'Something I heard,' he said slowly. 'From the other side.'

Helena nodded. Tears lingered in the corners of her eyes. 'Is my little girl okay? Down there, I mean... as okay as she could be?'

'I think she's made a friend,' Crane lied.

Helena smiled. After a moment she disappeared up the stairs, and for a few minutes Crane listened as the woman started to pack clothes neatly into thin, paper bags.

Maybe, now Elijah was the other side of the wall, he could find Ellen there too. Maybe they would keep each other company.

There was a nice thought.

Chapter Ten
THE OTHER SIDE

Elijah Davies was cold.

That was the first thing he noticed, when he woke up. It was *freezing*. He sat upright, his whole body shivering. He blinked. He felt... strange. Slowly, the boy stood up.

He was in a room. Or at least, it seemed like he was in a room. There were no walls, no floor. No ceiling. But it felt very much as though he was *inside* a room. He felt, if he tried to move very far, he would either reach some kind of impenetrable wall, or fall off the edge of this strange new world.

Everything was shadow. He had expected fire, burning torches miles high, a cavernous pit filled with demons and writhing flames and horrific, unnamed creatures. Instead, it was just... dark.

Not pitch-black, he noted, but a murky kind of grey. The shadows moved around him, floated in the nothing around his ankles, curled around the edges of the world which should have been very much invisible to him. Beyond the shadow and the shade, blinking on and off, faint, orange lights flew about the empty place like disembodied, amber eyes. Watching him.

'Hello?' he whispered. The shadows shifted, just a little, but there was no reply. Elijah noticed a smell now, that he hadn't before. It was that horrible sulphur smell again, but it was stronger here, and mixed with something else... something metallic.

Blood.

'Hello?' he said again, a little louder. 'Dad, are you here?'

No reply. Elijah stepped forward carefully – it was strange, walking on a floor that looked for all the world like it wasn't really there at all.

Elijah wondered how long he had been here. It felt as though he'd been asleep for a very long time. Years, perhaps. But he felt no older. In fact, he felt very little. He watched his feet move forward, but he could not feel his legs. He raised his arms, slowly, watched them tremble. But he couldn't feel them.

He listened.

He couldn't feel his own heartbeat.

The boy was panicking now, and he moved forward, squinting into the dark. 'Dad?' he called. 'Ellen? Is anyone here?'

'Shhh,' came a voice from behind him.

Elijah whirled round. Wide-eyed, afraid.

'Who's there?' he said. He could see nobody, in the shadows. He frowned. Turned, again, to keep walking.

Perhaps he'd imagined it.

The smell of blood grew stronger as he moved. He could hear it now, too, dripping...

'Who is that?' he hissed. 'Dad?'

Elijah paused. Stared into the shadows. Nothing but darkness and those eerie, orange lights. He shook his head.

Something reared out of the shadows, lunged for him, something with wide, terrible eyes and half a face, something spattered with red and carrying a shotgun -

'Shhh!' said the thing, grabbing Elijah's shoulders. The thing raised a crooked finger to its top lip. That was all that remained, it seemed, of the lower half of its face. The rest had been blown off and his jaw hung, bloody and oozing, before a mess of strings and a throat made of open flaps of skin. Elijah opened his mouth to scream, but the man with half a face clamped a hand over the boy's mouth, looking around them.

'You have to be quiet,' whispered the bloody man. 'He'll *hear* you.'

'Who?' Elijah said, voice muffled by the clammy palm of the thing before him.

'*Shhh!*'

Elijah nodded slowly. He looked the newcomer up and down. The man was dressed in a train conductor's uniform, but the uniform was covered in blood. There was a shotgun hung over one shoulder, crossing his back. It wasn't loaded. Half of the man's skull was squishy and raw and a constant trickle of red-pink ran down his back.

His eyes were glassy and dead.

'Are you... like me?' Elijah whispered.

The dead conductor nodded. 'Yes,' he hissed. 'No more questions. He's *listening*.' Quickly, he turned, gesturing for Elijah to follow him. The conductor walked quickly, passing through shadows as though he was used to all this, as though it was normal to him.

'How long have you been here?' Elijah whispered after a little while.

'I come and go,' the conductor said. 'Your friend... Mr Crane... said you'd need looking after. Said I should come and find you.'

Elijah paused. They walked on a little way.

'Is this Hell?'

The conductor stopped, turned around. 'Look,' he hissed. 'I'm trying to keep you... safe. No, this isn't Hell. Not yet. This is like... a waiting room, if you like. Like at the doctor's. Now, *no more questions*. The more you run your bloody mouth off, son, the more likely *he* is to –'

He stopped. There was something sticking out of his chest. Elijah swallowed.

'*Run...*' the conductor croaked.

Too late.

He fell to the ground and the thing in his chest

withdrew with a horrible, sticky sound like it was being dragged through a thick slab of raw, cold meat. The conductor convulsed on the shadowy ground for a minute before his eyes lit up a horrible, deep orange and he screamed, blood pouring from the new hole in his chest, arms twitching wildly.

Then he was gone, and the shadows took him away.

Elijah looked up.

The woman was tall, slim. Her dress was long and red and ragged. In a thin-fingered hand, she held something round and purple, something still *pulsing*. She looked down at the conductor's dead heart and grimaced, dropped it to the floor. The shadows swallowed it up and Elijah was completely alone with the woman in the red dress, and he screamed.

'Enough of that,' the woman said, and Elijah's throat closed up and he blinked.

'Now,' the woman continued. 'Elijah Davies. I believe you've met a good friend of mine. So tell me...'

She paused, and her eyes were on fire.

'What do you know about *Henry Crane?*'

Henry Crane leant back in the armchair, fingers wrapped around the handle of the poker. Beside him, the flames in the fireplace crackled quietly. Upstairs, Claire was still asleep. Slowly, the man turned his eyes toward the fire, stared into the flames. Above the hearth, the jackal's hollow eyes stared down at him.

Something brushed against his calf, and he looked down. 'Spider,' he said quietly. 'I thought you were keeping our guest company, no?'

The cat leapt up onto Crane's lap, gazed up at him with yellow eyes that glowed a little in the damp firelight. There was something in the cat's mouth. Crane frowned. He reached forward slowly, plucked the thing out from between Spider's pointed teeth. 'What have you brought me, huh?'

It was a tag, about half the size of his palm. 'Did you take this off Claire's box?' Crane asked quietly. He had seen it there earlier, tied to the brown paper with thin, frayed string, but he read it now for the first time.

He read it again.

'Oh, bollocks.'

Claire Kelly,
Wormwood House Orphanage
and Youth Shelter, London

'She's an *orphan*,' Crane whispered. 'Christ, Spider... what am I supposed to do now?'

The cat looked up at him blankly, and Crane shook his head. 'You have to take this back,' he said, and Spider took the tag in his mouth, held it neatly between his teeth. 'She can't know that we know, alright? Not until she's ready to tell us herself. Go on, now.'

Spider hopped off the man's lap and padded across

the living room, disappeared into the dark of the hallway. For a while Crane sat, staring into the fire. Eventually, he stood and dropped the poker into its place in the hearth, stuffed his hands into his pockets.

'Oh, what have I gotten myself into?'

He turned, then, and left the room, moved into the hall. Crossed the cement slabs quietly, headed up the stairs. Claire's bedroom door was open, and he glanced inside – Spider had slunk across the room and laid the tag down on the floor, beside the unwrapped brown paper box. The cat looked up as Crane passed, nodded his head. Yellow eyes dipped in the shadows.

'Good boy,' Crane whispered, and he kept walking.

He stopped at the grey door, raised his hand to the knob. It was quiet, beyond the door. Heat broke through the cracks in the wood, surged through the gaps between the door and the frame.

Crane turned the knob. 'It's only me,' he whispered. The door opened.

Warmth hit his face like a wave. A deep, orange glow threw light on him and he squinted into the room beyond, sheltered his eyes with the back of his hand.

'Good to see you too,' Crane said. 'It's been a while.'

He stepped forward, and the grey door closed behind him.

COMING SOON:

THE CASE FILES OF HENRY CRANE
BOOK TWO

A
TOWN
CALLED
HOPE

JACOB ALEXANDER

Printed in Great Britain
by Amazon